DISNEY'S
A Winnie the Pooh First Reader

Pooh's Four Seasons

Stories by Isabel Gaines

DISNEY
PRESS

NEW YORK

Contents

DISNEY'S
A Winnie the Pooh First Reader

Pooh's Easter Egg Hunt

by Isabel Gaines

ILLUSTRATED BY Studio Orlando

Pooh's Easter Egg Hunt

"Happy Easter!" Winnie the Pooh called to his friends.

They were all at Rabbit's house

for his Easter egg hunt.

"All right, everybody," Rabbit said.

"Whoever finds the most eggs wins.

Get ready . . . get set . . . go!"

Pooh, Piglet, Roo, Tigger,

Eeyore, and Kanga

ran into the woods.

9

Pooh found a yellow egg

under some daffodils.

He put the egg in his basket.

Poor Pooh didn't know

his basket

had a hole in it.

The yellow egg slipped out

and fell onto the soft grass.

11

Piglet found the yellow egg.

"Lucky me!" he said.

Then Pooh found a purple egg

behind a rock.

He put the purple egg

in his basket.

Oops! This egg slipped out, too.

Roo found the purple egg.

"Oh, goody!" he cried.

"Purple's my favorite color!"

Pooh found a green egg in a tree,

and put it in his basket.

He didn't see it fall back out.

Tigger found the green egg.

"Hoo-hoo-hoo!" Tigger cried.

"I'm on my way to winning!"

Next Pooh found a red egg . . .

that slipped through the hole

and into a clump of thistle.

Eeyore found the red egg.

"Surprise," he mumbled.

"I found an Easter egg."

On the side of a grassy hill,

Pooh found a blue egg.

"How pretty."

Pooh continued up the hill—

as the egg rolled down it.

Kanga found Pooh's blue egg

lodged against a log.

Finally, Rabbit shouted, "Time's up!"

Everyone gathered around.

"Let's see who won," Rabbit said.

Piglet, Roo, Tigger, Eeyore,

and Kanga showed their Easter eggs.

Pooh looked inside his empty basket.
"My eggs seem to be hiding again,"
he said.

Piglet looked at Pooh's basket.

"I think I know where," Piglet said,

poking his hand through the hole.

"You can have my yellow egg,"
said Piglet. "It was probably
your egg before it was mine."

"Thank you, Piglet," said Pooh.

"You can have my purple egg,

too," said Roo.

"Here, Buddy Bear," said Tigger.
"Tiggers only like to win
fair and square."

"Too good to be true," muttered Eeyore,
giving Pooh his red egg.

"And here's my blue egg," Kanga said.

"You're the winner, Pooh!"

Rabbit said.

"You win an Easter feast."

"Is there enough food

for my friends

to eat, too?" Pooh asked.

"I could make more,"

Rabbit said.

"Is there enough honey?" asked Pooh.

"There's plenty of honey," said Rabbit.

"Then let's eat!" said Pooh.

Everyone had a wonderful time.
Pooh enjoyed the food—
especially the honey!

Can you match the words with the pictures?

Kanga

basket

daffodil

purple

green

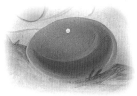

Fill in the missing letters.

P_oh

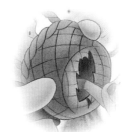

h_le

re_

_og

_oo

Disney's
A Winnie the Pooh First Reader

Pooh and the Storm That Sparkled

Adapted by Isabel Gaines

ILLUSTRATED BY Studio Orlando

Pooh and the Storm That Sparkled

BOOM! BOOM! BOOM-BOOM!

Pooh woke up with a start.

"What was that?"

There was a knock

at the door.

"Who's there?" said Pooh.

"Pooh, help!" a voice cried.

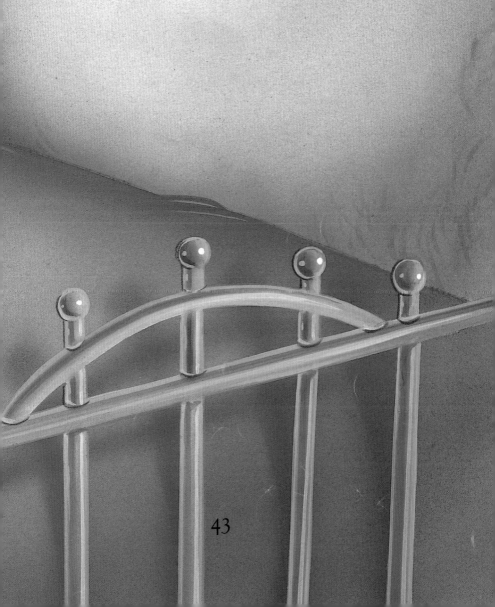

"Is that you, Piglet?"

"Yes!" said Piglet.

Pooh opened the door.

"A heffalump is after me!"
said Piglet.

"Where is it?" said Pooh.

"I don't know," said Piglet.

"I can only hear it."

BOOM! BOOM-BOOM! BOOM!

"The heffalump!" said Piglet.

Pooh looked out the door.

"Look!" said Pooh. "A red
flash! Now a white flash!
And a blue one!"

47

"Piglet," Pooh said,

"I believe your heffalump

is not a heffalump.

"It is a very bad storm.
What we hear is thunder
and what we see is lightning."
"I have never seen lightning
in so many colors," said Piglet.

"The storm is behind

the Great Hill," said Pooh.

"Oh dear," said Piglet.

"The last storm

blew Owl's house down."

"We better warn the others,"

said Pooh. "I'll get my honeypots."

BOOM! BOOM! BOOM! BOOM!

"What was that?" asked Owl.

He looked out his window.

He saw Pooh and Piglet

at his door.

"Owl," said Pooh,

"a big storm is coming."

"Here's a pot of honey
for you," said Pooh,
"so that you don't have
to go out for more food."

"Thank you, Pooh," said Owl.

"Let's warn Rabbit," said Pooh.

"A bad storm?" said Rabbit.

He looked up in the sky.

"But there are no clouds."

RABBITS
HOUSE

56

"That's because the storm

is still far away," answered Owl.

"It is a very bad storm," said Pooh.

BOOM! BOOM! BOOM! BOOM!

"Hear the thunder?" said Piglet.

"Rabbit, here's a pot of honey,"

said Pooh, "so that you

don't have to go

out for more food."

"Thank you, Pooh," said Rabbit.

"We have to warn Tigger," said Pooh.

"Tigger is not home," said Rabbit.

"He went on a picnic

with Kanga, Roo,

and Christopher Robin."

"B-B-But they will be near trees!"

cried Piglet.

"Christopher Robin told me

never to be near a tree

in a lightning storm!"

"We must save them," said Pooh.

"They are on the Great Hill,"

said Rabbit.

"The Great Hill!" cried the others.

"That is where the storm is!"

said Pooh.

Pooh, Piglet, Owl, and Rabbit

climbed the Great Hill.

The BOOMS got louder and louder.

The lightning was red,

green, gold, and blue.

It was round and sparkly

and made pretty patterns in the sky.

"I w-w-wish Christopher Robin

was here," cried Piglet.

They were at the top

of the hill.

They stopped short.

"What kind of storm

is this?" asked Pooh.

Christopher Robin ran

up to them.

"Happy Fourth of July!

Come watch the fireworks with us."

"But, Christopher Robin,"
said Pooh, "we've come
to save you from the storm."

"Silly bear," said Christopher Robin.

"It's not a storm.

They are fireworks!

Come join us."

And that's what they did.

"Oooo," said Pooh.

"Aaahh," said Piglet.

Can you match the words with the pictures?

Piglet

honeypot

tree

fireworks

Rabbit

Fill in the missing letters.

r_d

Kang_

do_r

hil_

b_ue

DISNEY'S

A Winnie the Pooh First Reader

Pooh's
Fall Harvest

Isabel Gaines

ILLUSTRATED BY MARK MARDEROSIAN AND TED ENIK

Pooh's Fall Harvest

It was a crisp and cool fall day.
The leaves had just begun
to change colors.

"Excuse me, Rabbit," said Pooh.

"We would love to help you

with your hardest,

but your hardest what?"

81

"No, Pooh," said Rabbit.
"I said 'harvest,' not 'hardest.'
It's fall—harvest season!"

"What is harvest season?"
asked Pooh.
"I only know winter,
spring, summer, and fall."

83

"Fall is the harvest season,"
said Christopher Robin.

"It's the time when
fruits and vegetables
in the garden become ripe."

"What does 'ripe' mean?"
asked Roo.

"It means
they are ready to eat,
dear," said Kanga.

"How do we tell
if they are ripe?" asked Piglet.
"Look for the vegetables
that look yummy," said Rabbit.

88

"They all look yummy," said Eeyore.

Rabbit knelt down

to look among the leaves.

He saw a tiny squash.

"No, Eeyore, this one is too small.
It has some more growing to do."

Owl picked a different squash.
"Not too big, not too little,"
he said. "This one is ripe."

"That's right, Owl,"
said Rabbit.

93

"Rabbit, what about this apple?"
said Pooh. "It looks yummy."

94

Pooh sat on a branch.

He was pointing to an apple

on the branch above.

Pooh reached for the apple.

95

But he lost his balance
and fell . . .
into Christopher Robin's arms.

"You had better leave
the apple picking to me,"
said Tigger, with a laugh.

Rabbit had lots
of wonderful foods
to be gathered.

He had sweet potatoes,
tomatoes, pumpkins,
and corn.

99

After all of it was collected,
Rabbit said, "I have more
than enough food
for this winter's storage.

So I would like
to invite you all
to a harvest celebration!"

Everyone left,

so Rabbit could prepare.

When they returned,
a long table was
covered with food.

They each took a seat,
except Rabbit,
who stood at the head
of the table.

"Thank you for helping me
with the fall harvest," he said.
"You are wonderful friends!"

Can you match the words with the pictures?

leaves

Rabbit

potatoes

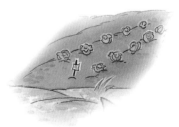

table

garden

Fill in the missing letters.

wi_ter

s_uash

ap_le

pu_pkin

R_o

Disney's
A Winnie the Pooh First Reader

Pooh's Christmas Gifts

by Isabel Gaines

ILLUSTRATED BY Mark Marderosian
and Fred Marvin

Pooh's Christmas Gifts

"Tomorrow is Christmas,"

said Kanga.

"And we're having a party!" said Roo.

"So please come to our house

at six o'clock," said Kanga.

"We want to celebrate

with all our friends."

"How fun!" said Pooh.

The next morning
when Pooh woke up,
it was dark outside.

"Oh my," he said.

"It must be six o'clock.

I'm late for the party."

Pooh hurried to Piglet's house.

When he arrived,

Pooh called out,

"Piglet, wake up.

We're late for the party."

Pooh and Piglet woke up

their other friends.

Then they all headed over

to Kanga and Roo's house.

"Merry Christmas!" yelled Pooh.

"Oh dear," said Kanga. "It is six o'clock in the morning!
I meant six o'clock tonight.

Please come back later,

and then we'll start the party."

Kanga and Roo closed their door.

"What are we going to do

until six o'clock tonight?" asked Pooh.

"Let's make a snowman," said Piglet.

They made three snowballs.

Then they stacked them

one on top of the other.

When they finished,

Tigger said,

"Let's make snow angels!"

They each found a spot

to lie down in the snow,

and then began flapping

their arms, legs, and wings.

Poor Eeyore had trouble

flapping his legs,

so he just rolled around on his back.

They all stood to admire their work.

Everyone's angel was perfect.

Except for Eeyore's.

His angel looked like a blob.

"I need to rest," said Eeyore.

Just then,

Christopher Robin walked by.

"I have a gift for each of you,"

he said.

"Why?" asked Piglet.

"Because on Christmas,

you give gifts

to those you love,"

said Christopher Robin.

"We should give
Christopher Robin a gift,"
said Rabbit.

"But what?" asked Tigger.

"I have an idea," said Pooh.

"Christopher Robin," said Pooh,

"we built this snowman.

And we would like

to give it to you

so you're never lonely."

"We made snow angels, too,"
said Piglet.

"We would like you
to have them, as well."

"So you never get lost,"

said Pooh.

"I am sorry mine looks

a little funny," added Eeyore.

"Thank you very much,"
said Christopher Robin.
"These are the best kinds of gifts
because they come from the heart."

"Kanga and Roo are giving us

a party," said Rabbit.

"What can we give them?"

asked Tigger.

"I know," said Owl.

"Let's give them a song."

Everyone agreed it was a great idea.

Pooh started the song,

and whenever he got stuck,

somebody would add a word.

Finally, they finished.

They practiced the song

until it was time for the party.

Then they went back

to Kanga and Roo's house,

and knocked on the door.

When Kanga and Roo opened the door,

all of their friends began to sing . . .

"We wish you a Merry Christmas.

We wish you a Merry Christmas.

We wish you a Merry Christmas,

Kanga and Roo.

"It's love that we bring

to share on this day

We wish you a Merry Christmas

with this song—Hurray!"

"This is the best gift ever!"
said Kanga. "Please come in
and enjoy the party."
And that's what all the friends did.